PROSPECT HTS. PUBLIC LIBRARY DISTRICT
W9-AWH-442

I LOVE MY BABY SISTER
(MOST OF THE TIME)

BY ELAINE EDELMAN · PICTURES BY WENDY WATSON

Lothrop, Lee & Shepard Books · New York

For my Mother and Father

—E.E.

 Inquiries should be addressed to Lothrop, Lee & Shepard Books, a division of William Morrow & Company, Inc., 105 Madison Avenue, New York, New York 10016. Printed in the United States of America. First Edition. 1 2 3 4 5 6 7 8 9 10

Library of Congress Cataloging in Publication Data

Edelman, Elaine. I love my baby sister (most of the time). Summary: A small girl looks forward to the time when her baby sister will be big enough to play with and be friends with. [1. Babies—Fiction. 2. Sisters—Fiction] I. Watson, Wendy, ill. II. Title. PZ7.E216Iad 1984 [E] 83-25623 ISBN 0-688-02245-6 ISBN 0-688-02247-2 (lib. bdg)

We have a new baby.

All she can say is *laa-laa, laa-laa.*
Sometimes she sings it,
so I sing along too.
She's my little sister.

She's fun to cuddle,
but I have to be careful.
My daddy says babies get hurt very easily.

But sometimes she yanks my hair,
and that hurts *me*.
I don't cry, though—
she's just a tiny baby.

Once I gave her a lollipop,

but she gave it back.

So I gave it back to her,

but she gave it back again.

So I ate it.

What a silly baby! When she's happy,
she laughs and makes funny noises.
Sometimes she makes mouth-bubbles. They're kind of sticky.

But when she's mad,

she screams worse than a hundred fire engines.

I don't like *that* at all.

She's too little to play my big-girl games.
Mostly, she just sleeps.
So I sing to her the way my daddy sings to me.
Good night, baby.
Sleep tight, baby.
Don't wake up 'til morning light, baby.

Sometimes my baby sister keeps Mother so busy

I have to jump around and holler, just to get a hug.

And when she eats, she does it so funny,
I have to wipe her nose and mouth for her.
Then, sometimes, she grabs my nose—ow!
My mother says she does that
because she loves me.

She'll be more fun
when she gets as big as me.
But then, I'll be a lot bigger too.

And I'll have to show her how to dress herself
and how to build with blocks.

We'll be friends
and hold hands
when we cross the street

and share our bikes and skates
and brush each other's hair....

And I might even let her button me
in the back, where I can't reach.

I hope my baby sister grows up soon.

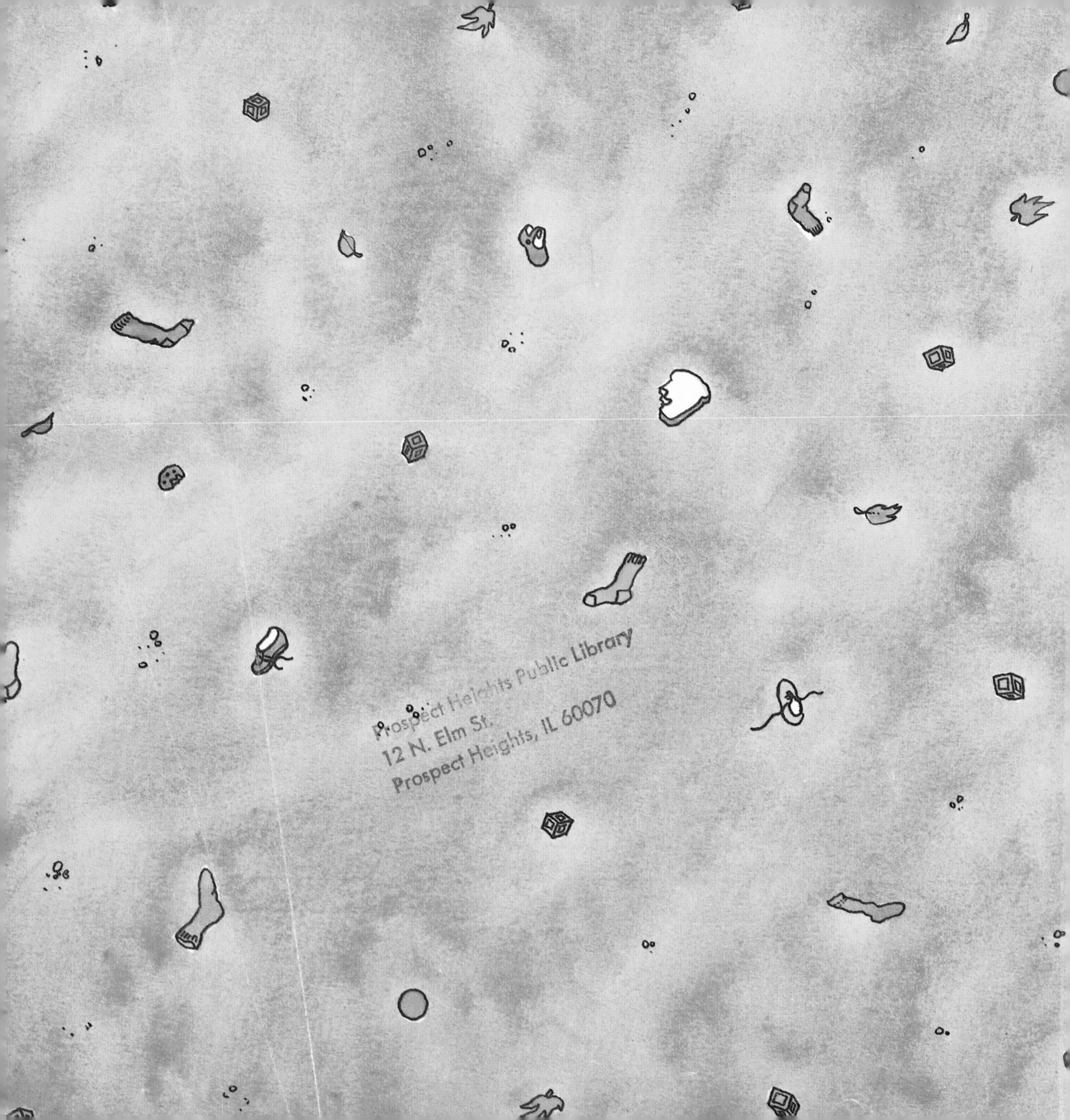